SUNNYSIDE
PRIMARY SCHOOL

INTO THE JUNGLE

For Barry and Joan

First published in Great Britain by
HarperCollins Publishers in 1993
First published in Picture Lions in 1993
Picture Lions is an imprint of the
Children's Division, part of
HarperCollins Publishers Ltd

Text and illustrations copyright
© Dennis Reader 1993

A CIP catalogue record for this title
is available from the British Library.

The author asserts the moral right to
be identified as the author of the work.

ISBN: 0 00 193755-3 (Hardback)
ISBN: 0 00 664280-2 (Picture Lions)

All rights reserved. No part of this
publication may be reproduced, stored
in a retrieval system, or transmitted
in any form or by any means, electronic,
mechanical, photocopying, recording or
otherwise, without the prior permission
of HarperCollins Publishers Ltd,
77-85 Fulham Palace Road,
Hammersmith, London W6 8JB.

Printed and bound in Hong Kong

This book is set in 18/22 New Baskerville

INTO THE JUNGLE

•Dennis Reader•

Collins

An Imprint of HarperCollinsPublishers

The house next door had stood empty for a long time.
As long as Jonathan Jones could remember.

One morning at breakfast Jonathan Jones's mother
made an important announcement. "We've got a jungle
explorer coming to live next door," she said.

A JUNGLE EXPLORER! Jonathan Jones couldn't wait.
It was so exciting. He could see him already. Just back
from tiger-crawling rain forests and snake-ridden swamps.

The day the jungle explorer moved in, Jonathan Jones
was at school. He hurried home that afternoon.
 There he was! In his garden! Wrestling with a lion, probably.

The jungle explorer was planting out a bed of mixed petunias.

He was very old and his name was Mr Stallebrass.

The only animals he had were a lot of fat, friendly cats.

"Are you *really* a jungle explorer?" asked Jonathan Jones.

"I used to be," said Mr Stallebrass, "until I ran out of
jungles to explore, but that was many years ago."

"What is it like, being an explorer?" asked Jonathan Jones.

"Just imagine," said Mr Stallebrass. "Just imagine the rockery is a mountain. Imagine the pond is a lake teeming with crocodiles... and over there the flowers and the weeds and the bushes are a steaming jungle."

Jonathan Jones stared hard. "I can see it all," he said.
"Then come with me," said Mr Stallebrass, "climb in
the boat, over the lake and into the jungle."

The boat journey was exciting.

"They're snapping well today," said Mr Stallebrass.

"Be brave. We'll be over in a jiffy."

The jungle was a wondrous place. It seemed to go on
for ever, full of wriggling snakes and jumping monkeys
and birds of paintbox colours.

And Mr Stallebrass's cats. Not fat curl-up-in-front-of-
the-fire cats but big, growling, lion cats.

There was even a friendly wild man who swung down
from the trees and told Jonathan that any friend of
Mr Stallebrass's was a friend of his.

"Jonathan and Mr Stallebrass have just paddled through the fish pond," said Mrs Jones.

"Now they're jumping about among the weeds," sniffed Mr Jones, who liked a nice neat garden.

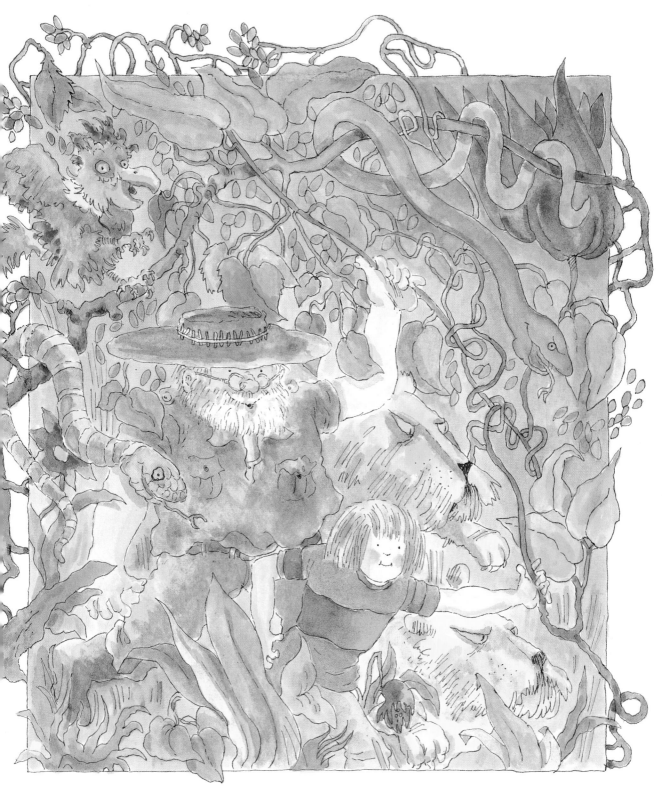

"What are we exploring for?" asked Jonathan Jones.
"The lost Temple of Gold of King Tutu," said
Mr Stallebrass. "He once ruled a civilisation of
enormous and fabulous wealth."

"There it is!" exclaimed Mr Stallebrass as they pushed through the undergrowth. "We've found the lost Temple. Now we shall both be famous."

"Your tea's ready," called Mrs Jones.

"There it is!" said Mr Stallebrass again. "Isn't it SPLENDID!"

"Let's go inside," said Jonathan Jones.

In the darkness there was a ghostly green glow.
"The fabulous emeralds of King Tutu," said
Mr Stallebrass. "Take them home for your mother
– and hurry. Your tea's ready."

"Mr Stallebrass sent you these," said Jonathan Jones.
"They once belonged to King Tutu."

"A basket of apples!" said Mrs Jones. "What a kind
old man Mr Stallebrass is."

The summer days that followed were long and filled
with magic. Exploring with Mr Stallebrass was the most
exciting adventure that had ever happened to Jonathan
Jones. He wanted it to go on for ever.

But towards the end of summer and just before the end of Jonathan's school holidays, Mr Stallebrass said he was tired and didn't really feel like another day's exploring.

Jonathan bravely went into the jungle on his own but it wasn't the same without Mr Stallebrass and his cats.

After that Mr Stallebrass didn't stay long in the house
next door. He left early one morning with a suitcase
and his cats. A van collected his furniture the next day.
Mrs Jones said he had gone to live with his sister.

The house next door was empty again. The tangled
weeds made the garden a lonely place.

If only Mr Stallebrass would come back. Mr Stallebrass
and his exciting adventures. Mr Stallebrass and his cats.

"Just imagine," he had said. "*Just imagine...*"
Jonathan Jones stared harder and harder.

Suddenly the garden was a magical garden again.
Something moved in the undergrowth. Perhaps all the
cats hadn't left with Mr Stallebrass. Jonathan Jones waved.
  And the lion gave a gentle purr.